WRITINGS FROM MY CORNER

Della Arms

Edited by Gary K Wallace

This book is a work of fiction. Names, characters, places, and incidents either are products of the author's imagination or are used fictitiously. Any resemblance to actual persons, living or dead, events, or locales is entirely coincidental.

Della Arms
Printed in the United States of America

First Printing: March, 2019
Makenlief.com

ISBN 978-1-73 38458-0-9

Dedication

To those of us who have lived to tell about it, and who, getting their second wind, are!

DELLA ARMS

Della didn't take writing seriously until after she was sixty. At that time, she began to write poetry, and has been published in a national magazine.

Art was her first love, but the duties of being a working single mother of three forced her to lay aside her brushes. She has won awards for her paintings and has had two one-woman shows. She will be combining her art and writing talents in this book.

Believing life doesn't necessarily begin at any particular age, or stop at one, Della is always open to new challenges. Publishing her work is her newest venture.

Acknowledgments

My gratitude to the San Marcos Library Writer's Group of whom I have many fond memories. Many thanks to the writer's group and the friends who were most helpful in creating this book. Also, special thanks to my friends and family who both inspired and encouraged me in my artistic pursuits.

My deepest appreciation goes to my son Kevin Paul who at the tender age of 13 recognized my talent and encouraged me. He was the spark that lit my creative fires. Those fires have burned bright for many years.

My heartfelt gratitude to Gary Wallace whose idea started this whole project. His concepts and insights brought this small volume of my writings about life, love, and nature to light.

CONTENTS

Part I
Short Stories

Almost Enchanted 1949

STAY THROUGH CHRISTMAS

"Stay through Christmas," she begged, choking on the rage and fear that suffocated her. How dare he leave, to leave at all, right before Christmas? She had crumpled to the floor, clinging to his legs, inconsolable. It was painful knowing how much he wanted to go. His side of the closet bare, his drawers empty.

Mitch gently ran his hand through her hair. "Kara, Kara, get up. Tears won't change anything."

In the back of her mind, she remembered taking the mugs from the small table and started out of the room. "Damn him. Oh, damn him. Our life has always been on his timetable—their children, their friends, vacations, now this." She turned and hurled a mug barely missing Mitch's head, surprising them both.

"All right, Kara." He sighed. "All right, I'll stay through Christmas. I'll stay under the condition you'll have the Christmas stuff put away by New Year's Eve. Your new life starts then, January first." He leveled his weary eyes at her. "This January, in four weeks."

God, how am I going to do this? she thought. Mitch was a master at organizing and planning. For sixteen years he called every shot. Now, he was leaving, and she had never even learned how to shoot.

Kara put the last tissue wrapped ornament in the storage box and taped it shut. A gaily wrapped gift looked misplaced leaning against the wall behind the tree. A card attached to the top read: Don't open until New Year's Eve.

The tree looked naked. The string of lights appeared to cling desperately to the dried branches. Kara couldn't bear to remove them yet. She reached to plug the lights into the wall socket, knocking the mug of cider off the footstool. Her eyes welled with tears, remembering the other mug. The three weeks before Christmas had been tough. But this week, without Mitch, was the hardest week of all.

Christmas Eve had been joyous. The home movies of their children's earlier years kept the mood lite and fun. They watched the rest on Christmas Day. The evening meal had been difficult. Their favorite foods hardly touched. It was mentioned, but understood, Mitch would leave the next day.

Kara picked up the shattered pieces and headed for the kitchen to get another cup of cider. She took it to the darkened balcony, glad the children were with their grandparents.

Kara listened to the sounds of the night. Tracker, the overindulged boxer of her neighbor, whined to be let in. Black Jack, Kara's big Maine coon cat, who wasn't black at all, was raising a ruckus to be let out. The laughter of the Jenkin's New Year's Eve party, followed by the refrains of Auld Lang Syne, sent Kara back to the tree and the unopened gift. It was New Year's Eve.

She removed the candy-striped bow, then the lid. Inside the box were two books. A letter lay on top. It read: Darling Kara, thanks for the best years of my life. Tomorrow you too will be on a new path, as I'm on mine. One journal is for you to write to me about all the things you never got to say. Write about all the things you wish could have been and can never be. Or whatever else that suits you. The other journal is for a daily account of the steps you are taking toward the next chapter of your new life.

"I'm glad you made me stay through Christmas," he whispered to her before the machines keeping him alive were unplugged.

Kara wanted to hit something, to scream, to cuss, to cry out. Hugging the books close to her chest she swallowed hard. With tears rolling down her cheeks, her hand trembling, Kara leaned over and unplugged the Christmas Lights.

BEHIND THE MASK

Margo patted another layer of makeup on her cheek to mask the bruise. She turned her face sideways to check the results.

"That should do it," she said, "One would have to look close to see the discoloration."

Margo had been hiding behind a mask most of her life, careful not to show the pain. It started with her sibling's ridicule and put-downs. "Smile and ignore them," her mother told her. It hadn't stopped their attacks, though. Frustrated by Margo's lack of response, they would escalate until one of their parents would intervene and send them to their room. Of course, it became Margo's fault they got into trouble.

In Junior high, it had worked well. Margo called the smile 'her secret'. When she was permitted to wear lipstick, her mother had told her, after you put on your lipstick, put on your smile and keep it there, then lift an eyebrow and walk away."

Learning to lift only one brow had been difficult but was worth it. In school, when the posh girls would taunt her, Margo smiled, arched a brow, and walked away. It drove them wild. They wanted to know what she was smiling about. They wanted to know what she knew that they didn't. Knowing their bewilderment and frustration, made Margo smile on the inside. Sometimes she would laugh before lifting a brow and walking away.

She wouldn't tell her best friend, I'm just thinking about my secret. She didn't trust her. Loyalty was a thing Margo didn't think Mary Martha understood. Margo's own brothers and sisters sure hadn't. Her younger sister would make up things to get her in trouble with her dad. Her brother, also younger, would 'rat her out' on a minute's notice.

The bird nests were the worst betrayal. Their dad destroyed all the bird nests. When Margo would find one and wanted to share her discovery with someone, she told her brother. Then she discovered he would tell their dad.

In college, her permanent smiles created a mystic. She never explained things, nor could she be pulled into any petty conflicts. They weren't worth her time. And it was true, other people spent a lot of time and energy on things that were none of their business. Their involvement seldom solved or made anything better. In the workplace and in her first marriage she kept her own counsel and kept others out, staying safe behind her smile. It became her way of life.

This was different, a bruise you couldn't smile and walk away from. It went with you. She could say; I walked into a door or missed catching the ball. Margo could start laughing or she could say, Allen had hit her. He would laugh and say, one of these days Alice, one of these days and everyone would laugh. Maybe, just maybe she should make up an outrageous tale and have fun with it. No one would believe the truth anyway; that she'd been hit by a twenty-pound piñata at her son's birthday party.

CAMOUFLAGED LIES

The light through the stained-glass windows distorted the faces of the choir. It was surreal. I stood with my mother, across from the preacher and the family. We were watching the mourners as they moved past. The second-grade teacher, her heavily powdered face streaked with tears, moved up to Mr. Wyatt and patted his arm.

"This too will pass," she said.

Dumfounded, I turned to my mother and whispered loudly, "Why is she saying Mrs. Wyatt has already passed!"

A gloved hand covered my mouth. Mom whispered in my ear, "Just be quiet, we'll talk about this later."

WRITINGS FROM MY CORNER

Stepping behind Mom, so Mr. Wyatt couldn't see me, I watched and listened as the mourners filed by sobbing and mumbling. In a dark print dress, Mrs. Pruitt stepped up and said in a low voice, "I'm sure it's all for the best."

Horrified, I stared after her. Janie and her brother didn't have a mother anymore. That is for the best? There was something wrong here. Only old people died not someone as young as my mother. That's not right, not right at all, I fumed, squirming. Mom pinched my shoulder to still me.

At the cemetery, spurts of wind tossed the turned dirt around and up into our faces. Janie said it was her mother being really mad.

"Yeah," I said. "I'd be mad too if I was dead."

Mr. Wyatt shushed us.

At the house, there was more food laid out than we'd had at the church's July 4th picnic. Only a few children were there, school friends and cousins, who sat with their parents. I took my plate with a buttermilk biscuit, a chicken wing, and potato salad out to the backyard leaving my lemonade glass in the kitchen sink. I gave the dog the biscuit, settled myself in the tire swing to eat.

The dog reached for my chicken wing, during the scuffle the potato salad slipped from my plate and landed on my polished shoes. The dog gobbled it off taking a button with it. I stared at the spot where the button had been thinking, nobody is gonna believe this.

Pushing the hard ground with my feet, the swing moved back and forth. I puzzled over what I had heard. Mr. Russell had said when one door closes another door opens. What did that have to do with Mrs. Wyatt being dead? Besides everybody's house was the same. When you closed one door, you had to open another to get out of the room.

On the way home, I thought of the song we sang in Sunday school, *Jesus loves the little children of the world.* He didn't love the Wyatt children very much. He took away their mother.

There were starving Armenian children somewhere who would have loved the boiled okra I gagged on. I couldn't understand why I had to eat it if they wanted it. And the Mexican children who didn't have homes, they lived in shacks on the riverbank. They didn't have shoes either.

Mom tried to explain what Miss Barger had meant about 'this too will pass' telling me nothing good lasts forever and dear, bad stuff doesn't last forever either.

Trying not to cry, I sputtered, "I know, it just gets out of the way for more bad stuff to happen."

A lot of bad stuff had happened, and dead was dead. My kitten was dead. It wasn't coming back. The new cat didn't stop me from missing the dead one. I was in a dark mood and couldn't be consoled. Exasperated, Mom told me I would put her in an early grave. That jolted me out of my state of despondency. I didn't want to be like Janie and not have a mother anymore.

The man on the neighboring farm beat up his wife, she nearly died and lost her baby. I wanted to know where God was and why he wasn't protecting her, a good Christian woman. She went to church, he didn't.

"Her husband did a lot of mean stuff, and nothing ever happened to him," I shouted.

"Everything happens for a reason," Mom said.

In a loud voice, I continued my tirade. "What kind of God is that, who lets good people get hurt and nothing happens to the bad people who hurt them?"

"Mom turned to Dad. "Carrol, help me out here."

Dad looked at Mom, got up from the table and left his dinner unfinished.

"Holly, you take her to church—you handle it," he said and left the house.

I started to follow, but Mom gave me that *look*. I remembered dad didn't go to church either. That scared me, I couldn't finish my dinner.

I had heard the church pianist say one morning everything happens for a good reason for those who love God.

"Nita's baby died, and she got beat up, and that's a good reason?" I challenged.

"Honey, that's part of God's plan and I don't know God's plans." She sighed and looked away and whispered, "God has a plan for everyone."

What Mom said scared me. God's plan for me might be bad too. Terrified, not knowing what to do, what to think or who to talk to, I backed out of the room. Leaving the house, I ran down to the barn with my dog close at my heels. With tears running down my face, I climbed the rail fence and whistled for my horse. Climbing on her bare back, I rode until dark.

God has a plan for everyone. It's God's plan that a person is to be murdered? It's God's plan that the Mexican children don't get homes and have to live down by the river? It's God's plan that some babies are born with funny faces and twisted legs?

Six years later I sat for the last time in the little church. The afternoon sun coming through the stained-glass windows gave the choir a comic look. It was Charlie Taylor, the town drunk's funeral. Dad was a pallbearer. This was the only time I ever saw him in church. A month later we left for California. On the way, I pondered the "God stuff". It still made no sense. "God gives us free will" angered me the most. Tell that to Janie's mother or to Nita, I thought, or the Armenian children who would have eaten my boiled okra or the Mexican children who didn't have homes or shoes. I doubt they had a choice to choose the circumstances in which they had to live. I didn't know about the rest of the world yet. Or the word hypocrisy what it meant.

The adult wisdom I grew up with made little sense then. Most of it rankles me to this day. As a child 'don't rock the boat' drove me wild. It implied that some people got to live by a different set of rules. If the banker's daughter lied and got someone else in trouble you weren't supposed to say anything. If the sheriff's son stole something, and you saw it, you kept quiet. I wasn't good at keeping quiet and mom would throw the 'early grave' guilt trip on me. Another falsehood that can send me into orbit is: 'What goes around comes around'. That applies to the common cold and little else.

When we are having a rash of little girls kidnapped, raped, molested, and murdered. I couldn't accept it all 'happened for the best' or be comforted to hear 'this too will pass' or 'when a door closes another door opens. Their loved one sure wouldn't be on the other side of it.

When unjust things happen, you are told that it shouldn't be any of your concern. So, "don't rock the boat means" look the other way and let it happen. Sure, this incident will pass because what goes around comes around but left alone it will fester and become dangerous, like the Columbine school massacre. Surely, that didn't 'happen for the best'. Things upset me that people spouted out the truth as the cure-all.

"You can't change things," my sister said. "So, don't get involved."

"And why not? I asked.

"Well, first off," she came back at me, "you keep this up and you'll have Mom spinning in her grave."

Her answer had nothing to do with what we were talking about. To let things, go or to polish over them with some inane babblings is a copout. I can't for the life of me believe the service men and women who died or were maimed in Iraq or their loved ones would buy into the babble. My sister, married fifty years to a navy man, has an arsenal of platitudes to cover/explain away every situation. She becomes annoyed when she thinks she's being challenged and goes for the guilt technique that Mom used on me.

"I don't think Mom will get any eternal rest until you die," she told me.

"And neither will you," I snapped. "So, be glad I too will pass. And in the meantime, I'll rock the boat as much as I can, and it'll all be for the best.

SHE'LL BE WEARING RED

"She'll be wearing red, Paul."

"Everyone wears red," I yelled at my sister,

"Not like she does, nobody wears red as she does. Oh, by the way, you'll love her sense of design. Look, I'm running late, see you there"

"Hey…" I sputtered at the dial tone. "I don't have a good feeling about this. It's not safe to be comfortable with anything Claire plans or does for that matter. I'd like her sense of design. What in the hell did she mean by that parting shot?"

Twenty minutes or so later, in a bad mood, a glass of wine in my left hand, and a list of the artists in my right. I sat in the far corner diagonal from the entry next to a small plate of assorted cheese and crackers. The food and drink bar to my left made surveillance easy.

I had agreed to let Claire get me a date for the formal family reunion dinner my cousin was throwing. On the condition, I got a good look at her first. This artist reception was designated as the place for checking out my prospective date.

I wondered if the lady I was watching out for, was one of the ones Claire had tried to fix me up with before. Every time I'm in town she has someone she wants me to meet. Last time I was here, I wasn't into meeting a gal of any kind. I was too busy scrambling my way out of a relationship I should not have been in, in the first place. The time before that, I was pursuing something I didn't want to mess up. I didn't like Claire's funky friends, never did and tried to stay clear of them.

I'd been pretty successful until my cousin Kit came up with this black-tie sit-down family reunion affair. She had scribbled at the bottom of the summons to bring a date. She didn't want odd numbers at her tables.

If it hadn't been the five-year reunion, I wouldn't have let anyone know I was in town but Mom and Dad. Being the youngest of nine from a good Catholic family, I was one of two boys. "Bookends," Mom called us. I felt smothered by seven sisters and countless girl cousins. A comfortable relationship with a female has not been on my list of accomplishments. Out of college, I'd put as much distance from family as I could, like on the other coast.

I was right, everyone seemed to be wearing red. I was looking for a small, witty female wearing red like nobody else did. She'd be alone. A tall girl in a red dress walked through the door and headed to the wine table, definitely not her. Huge red handbag and matching shoes came in—too old. A woman with a red skirt and matching vest was definitely with someone. I scanned the room again. Indeed, just about everyone wore something red, but nothing out of the ordinary.

I sipped my wine and waited for Claire. God, how many times in these many, many years have I waited for Claire? I didn't want to think about it. I didn't want to think about tomorrow night and what she had cooked up this time. No use calling her back. She wouldn't pick up. My eyes rested on the backside of neatly filled out blue jeans. The lady wore a matching jacket and purse swung over her shoulder—nothing red there that I could see. I liked what I saw, from the casual hairstyle to the medium heeled sandals. The group was laughing at something she had said, giving her a high five.

More people entered the gallery, mostly women. I wondered if the few males who were here were one of the artists or a husband of an artist? It was obvious people knew each other. The neat set of buns had moved on to another group of people, and I got a good look at her profile. I liked that too. Damn, she wasn't wearing red that I could see. She didn't appear attached to any one person or group either.

Where in the hell was Claire? She is the sister eleven months, twenty-nine days, four hours and a few minutes older than I am. It beats the hell out of me why Claire has it down to the minute, but she does. . . anal, typical of her.

Annoyed, I glanced at my watch it wasn't as late as I thought. The place was filling up, the noise level high, the jeans nowhere in sight. Five more minutes, I thought, then I'm outta here, no date, no dinner.

I looked around for a place to dump the cheese and wine. Seeing none, I decided to finish them off and then a lady in red sashayed in. Oh my god, she was alone. She was short, vivacious, and wearing red—everything red. A flimsy dress, shoes, large tote and, my god, red legs? I didn't realize I was choking until someone began banging me on the back. They took my empty wine glass and handed me a wad of napkins.

"You look like someone who needs rescuing," she said. "Quick, this way."

For a second, I looked into eyes bluer than her jeans. With a firm grip on my elbow, she guided me around the crowd, out the front door, and across the street. We flopped into chairs in a sidewalk café. I was still coughing, sweating more than just a little from my narrow escape, muttering, "I was going to kill Claire this time for sure"

Laughter brought me to my senses. "You must be Paul, Claire's baby brother," she said.

It was the lady in blue jeans with a neat set of buns.

"Huh," I choked out.

"You're Paul, Claire's brother?"

"Yeah," I managed," how did you know?"

Laughing she handed me a glass of water and waved away the waitress. It was then I noticed she wore red. A plain silk shell, her necklace was a work of art in itself, difference sizes, shapes, and shades, of red. A wide belt, yes red, an unusual design cinched her waist. Stunning, unusual. That's when it hit me. No one wore red like she did. That's when what Claire had said hit me, "I would like her sense of design." The cut of the jeans and the jacket were different. Incredible I wished half of my employees had that sense of style, what to put together and how.

Dazed I settled back in my chair and took in this vision across from me. "How did you know I was Claire's brother?" I ask again.

"Oh, she described you pretty well, besides she showed me that picture of you."

"She didn't. Of course, she did, and I am going to kill her."

"Claire said you'd lose it when you saw Vera. So, I came early for the show."

"I should have guessed. Claire set this charade up—didn't she?

"Well, yeah, sorta." Her hand slipped up to hide the smirk.

"You were in on it, weren't you? This whole thing?"

"I plead the fifth," she laughed.

"I bet Vera was in on this too. What she was wearing was too outrageous to be believable"

"You sound like a fashion critic"

"With seven older sisters, I knew about fashion before I knew there was football, which has been most helpful in my business."

"I can't believe that either of you is friends of Claire's. She's a practical joker but this was overkill, even for Claire. There must something I am missing here."

"Well, for one thing, I wanted a good look at you before I agreed to the date."

"The date? You wanted a look at me before you agreed to the date?"

"The formal, sit down dinner, tomorrow night, at your cousins"

"Oh, really now, and the other thing?"

"Setting you up sounded like it would be too much fun to miss out on."

"Alright, I'll hand you that, but now it's 'get even time'. Game for some more fun?"

"Like what?"

"Um... let's see...ah. Look. I want you to tell Claire when she gets here, that I took one look at Vera and bolted out the door and tell her you were so embarrassed that you wouldn't be caught dead in the dark with me.

But I wasn't embarrassed—"

"I know. I know. It's payback time"

"You wouldn't? She'll lose it, you know."

"Yeah. This's so sweet" I rubbed my hands together. "You're fine with a tux and tie tomorrow night?"

"Yeah, I am, providing Claire doesn't catch on and kill us both first."

"I'll let my cousin in on the joke she'll love it." Holding back a laugh, I sighed.

"I better get back to the reception before Claire arrives. She wrote on a napkin her address and handed it to me. She'll pick me up here around 7:15. Oh, by-the-way, I'll be wearing red," laughing she ran back across the street.

"Oh shit, Claire will love this. I didn't even get her name.

THE RED SHOES

Going through the dusty old trunk on a cold, rainy day, opened up another world for Susanne.

The red sequined dancing shoes wrapped in brittle tissue paper was a surprise. This was Gran Nan's trunk she was rummaging through. Her grandmother had married much too young to ever have studied dance seriously much less danced professionally.

Later she asked her Aunt Jane about them. Her aunt, youngest of Gran Nan's three children, was as surprised as Susanne, saying she had no clue. Uncle Joe was of no help either. No one else in the family was able to shed any light on the mystery.

Susanne thought one of Gran Nan's diaries might shed some light on the red shoes. She was right. After many hours, she found the entry written in Gran Nan's own hand. It read: *I put my red shoes on maybe for the last time. Jane's getting too heavy to carry. She's the third of my babies I've danced to sleep. Joe and Joan weren't this heavy at two.*

Susanne thought they knew all there was to know about Gran Nan. Grandpa Tyler and Gran Nan were neighbors. He was three, when, after four boys, the Wilsons finally had a girl. Tyler had never seen a girl baby and wondered what one looked like. Babies, he had thought, were little kids who hadn't learned to walk yet. This baby was tiny, about the size of one of his big sister's dolls. Her parents named her Nancy.

Her brothers said her name was bigger than she, so they called her little Nan. Tyler had gazed down enthralled at the sleeping baby. He leaned over the edge of the bassinet and kissed her cheek, then whispered, "When we both get bigger, we're going to get married."

Everyone, family and community alike, thought that was just about the cutest thing they had ever heard. They all thought it was adorable, her brothers and their friend, took Little Nan with them almost everywhere they went. Tyler was the one who pushed the stroller, righted her tricycle, and held her hand.

For the next seventeen years, they saw each other every day. Tyler had turned down a basketball scholarship from the State University because it was too far away from Nan. He attended the local junior college instead.

Then WW II intervened. When Grandpa got drafted, they wanted to get married, so Nan could go and live where he would be stationed. This created a family crisis. Gran Nan wasn't seventeen.

Gran said she'd run away if they didn't let her. Her parents, who had never experienced the tough side of little Nan, were shocked. Her brothers and Tyler weren't, though. They had seen her, at five, take on Danny Tolson, the neighborhood bully. He had tied a can to a cat's tail. Then she turned her fury on her brothers and Tyler for laughing about it. There was no peace until the cat was found and fed tuna for a whole week. She had insisted they buy the tuna with their own money

Tyler and Nan were married two weeks after her seventeenth birthday. Boot camp separated them for the first time.

It was common knowledge Gran Nan liked to dance. She had taken lessons and taught Grandpa Tyler a few steps. They starred at ballrooms. If there was a dance contest they won, it. But dance professionally? The shoes were well worn and dancing her children to sleep didn't include Grandpa Tyler. Where and how did the shoes become such a big part of her life and not be attached to him?

The garage was the last area Susanne cleared of her grandparent's home. In the rafters was Grandpa Tyler's footlocker. In it was a fat stack of letters tied with twine, written in the precise backhand she recognized. Suzanne found what she was hoping for. After reading most of them, she uncovered the one that solved the mystery.

The letter read: *Sweetheart, I love, love, love the shoes. I'll wear them while I'm dancing little Joe to sleep. I'll pretend I am Dorothy and he is Toto. How sweet of you to remember our first movie. It was the first time we went anywhere without my big brothers. Nobody caught on. Mom would have had a fit if she had. I was only 13. Miss you much, love you a lot. Until we can dance together again, your Dorothy. Love, Kisses and a bushel of hugs, Nan.*

THE LONG WAIT

The little girl sat on the edge of the step, second down from the top. A gentle breeze rocked the porch swing enough to invoke a rhythmic squeaking. She darted a quick glance its way before she turned her watchful eye to the yard.

Fallen leaves danced across the cracked cement—some caught on the thorns of leafless rose bushes. Tilting her face upward, her eyes scanned the barren branches for the fifth time, seeing only a crow perched there, calling to the others circling above.

Her eyes dropped to her lap as she ran her fingers through its contents. She shook the strands of her sun-bleached hair that fell across her face as she watched the kittens scamper along the white picket fence, one jumping to the ground to chase a dancing leaf, another climbing the crow filled tree.

The peeling fence kept out most of the neighborhood dogs that chased the squirrels every chance they got. A few squirrels had come out on the limbs to watch the activity below.

The child stretched her legs in front of her and bounced down the remaining steps. The kitten's mother came over and rubbed up against her leg, purring. Carefully folding her skirts over its contents, she climbed to the top step, giving herself a better view of the yard.

A squirrel scampered down the tree trunk, only to return, to the lowest branch scolding the barking dog below.

Time passed, the postman came, leaving mail in the box by the gate. The children next door came home for lunch. She hunkered down behind the porch post, not wishing to be seen, not willing to subject herself to their taunting.

Her mother came out and urged her to come in saying, "Honey, Pesky isn't with us anymore." The child rose, letting the contents of her skirt bounce down the steps. She turned at the door to watch the squirrels and crows descend on them from the tree. "Maybe Pesky did go south last week, so I guess the other squirrels can have his peanuts."

Fighting back tears, she went in and closed the door behind her.

THE OTHER SIDE

I surveyed my morning's work. The plants that didn't make it through the winter were removed. Others needing more space were divided and repotted. Pony packs of petunias, periwinkles, and marigolds in their new pots. I placed the extras by the front door for Kay. I phoned her. "Help, I have plants looking for a home."

She laughed and said, "She would rescue them in an hour or so."

The garden, my retreat, my special place was beautiful. I created it in the northwest corner of the small balcony. The 3 by 8 foot "L" bleacher style had three rows of shelving loaded with potted flowers and herbs; rosemary, thyme, and basil. A miniature Japanese Tea tree stood at one end. A small birdbath stood at the other. The wind chimes swayed on a gentle breeze and tinkled.

A new hummingbird feeder had its first visitors. Territorial little creatures, four were fighting over it. The wild bird feeder had been washed and refilled with seeds. Sparrows and house finches would be along shortly. A dish of seed on the top shelf of my bleacher garden waited for the doves—they were too big for the swinging feeder.

I headed for the table and chairs at the far end of the balcony. There I had spent many hours, my cats beside me, enjoying the birds and butterflies that visited our garden. Other times, reading or listening to music, my cats curled beside me, asleep.

Both are gone now. After fourteen years Puff left, four years later Trouble joined him on the other side. Their leaving left a hole in my life, yet to be filled.

The ice in my tea had melted. I put the glass back on the table and opened the bag of bread pieces ready to toss into the air for the crows and seagulls. I stood for a moment to watch the gulls pulling garbage bags from the dumpster three stories below. Tearing them apart, they searched for scraps, only to have a crow dive from the roof to steal them. My cats had spent hours watching this circus.

The sky was overcast. One could hear the airplanes, but not see them. The police helicopter lower and circling. I tossed the bread, then returned to my chair.

Jerking awake, I became aware of my surroundings. Something was different, but the same. I was surprised that the plants seemed larger, the flowers in fuller bloom. The finches no longer fought over the seeds, but dozens of them sat lined up on the balcony rail. The Eucalyptus tree was loaded with crows. Two mockingbirds sat atop a flowering bush, silent and still. A red tail hawk perched on the light standard in the parking lot. Seagulls in scattered stillness stood on the tarmac.

The "still" was confusing. Even the air felt still. Not stifling, just still. The sky, an incredible blue. I heard no cars, focusing, I saw none. Was that Kay ringing the doorbell, knocking on my door, calling my name? Starting to get up I became aware of the cats in my lap purring. How could this be? They crossed to the other side years ago.

Puff reached to touch my face. I stared, trying to understand the strangeness of it all. Reality set in. Stunned, I realized, I too, was on the other side.

Kittens sketch on scrap paper 1950

LITTLE DOG

I was halfway to the door to open it before I realized you were no longer with us. I stood listening for the sound again, knowing I would not hear it but so wanting to. Was it the wind in your absence that rattled the door to keep your memory alive? It needn't have, the dear little dog of doubtful heritage. You are as real in our hearts as if you still romped among us.

You taught us love—unconditional love. You loved us even when the children forgot to put food or fresh water out for you. When baseball, scout troops, or other activities took us away. Even when we gave less of ourselves, you never complained. You were always there with your love and devotion, demanding nothing, but giving so much.

For eleven years you taught the children, mine, and the neighborhood about birth, love, then about death. The gathering for your wake was surprising and unsurpassed. I watched as the boys, long since too big to cry, stood with their hands in pockets, as near to you as they could, remembering.

Once you treed the gasman who came unwittingly into the yard while it was filled with playing children. You wouldn't let the astonished man down until all were safe inside. Afterward, you greeted your now weary friend, in your usual tail wagging way. An angry parent thought twice about spanking their child in your presence. Many a little scoundrel sought safety in your house until the heat was off.

Arnold, the neighborhood bully, aside from the others, looked at where you were. I wondered if he remembered the time he ran away, all of a block from home, to live with you. He tearfully said, "You loved him and understood him when no one else did."

I wonder, little dog if you didn't wipe away as many of the children's tears as their mothers had. So many times, you stood patiently while a little one told you how mean their mommies and daddies were, their tear-streaked faces buried in your fur.

They loved you best of all for never disclosing their hiding places when playing hide and seek. Nor would you "out them" when their pockets were filled with cookies. You seemed to know they wouldn't forget you. Patiently, inside your house with your head on paws, you would wait, watching until they slipped you one.

Autumn was your time of year. Delighted, you chased the dancing leaves as they fell. No pile was safe. You plowed through or buried yourself in them. From this vantage point of the leaves, you watched the activity of the yard. If someone should come near, you defended your hiding place like a bear. We would leave the leaves until the last minute before bagging them. That is where you slept, cuddled close until they were hauled away.

I think of the other times you slept in the house but under the window of one child recovering from chicken pox or measles.

Your toys, I look at them now where you left them. You always carried them back when you were through playing. I never understood how you learned it without training and my children with all theirs never did. The rope, which in the last days you still brought over wanting to play was still there. The years have taken their toll and after a tug or two, you would lay your head in the lap of your opponent as if to apologize for not giving them a good game.

I wipe tears from my face as I remember the other games, I was too busy to take time to play. I can hear in my mind the plunk of the tennis ball on the driveway where you dropped it sat and watched it roll away. Balls twice your size you would push around the yard like a seal, then toss them in the air. If you had an audience, like a child seeking attention, you'd choose the largest ball, butting it around, then jump over it.

Shoes left lying around, there were many, you never touched, which amazes me still. Did you have some built-in understanding they were 'untouchables'? Worn out jeans were your favorite toy dragging them around, sleeping with them, tearing them to shred. The neighborhood kids kept you well supplied. Their moms suspected foul play when their children's new ones appeared past repair. You didn't like them anymore once they were washed.

We kept none of your puppies, there were many, to the delights of the neighborhood children. We wished we had. You trained them well. I wished I had been as successful as a parent like you. The puppies were a marvel and had no trouble finding loving homes.

I remember the first puppy you lost. We were stunned when you dug it up from its resting place, cleaned it, and hid it under your body. Not until we wrapped it in flannel as we had done with the weak ones from other litters were you content to let it be. It rests today in another yard not far away. We hope you are romping together somewhere safe and happy because of little dogs such as you, so full of love, must never stop being.

THE WOMAN AND THE DOG

The dog appeared before the first frost. It lay near a scrawny bush right off the path to the outhouse. He seemed bewildered and wary. With his head on his forepaws, he watched the woman's every move. It looked half wolf, which made no sense, as there were no wolves in this part of the country nor had there been, for more than the woman's years. It looked hungry, but not starved. His coat suggested he had been well cared for in the not too distant past.

The woman put off the inevitable trip as long as she could, waiting for the dog to move on. But it didn't. The shade of the bush disappeared when the sun reached midday point in the cloudless sky. The dog stayed put. He pushed his body as close as he could to the small branches seeking relief from the heat. It made no movement when the woman returned from the outhouse. She continued to ignore him.

On the second day, the woman placed a cake tin under the dripping joint of the pipe running from the windmill. On an earlier trip to fetch house water, she noticed the ground had been scratched and licked. As far as the woman knew, the dog had not moved from the bush. It had dug a hole down to the roots in search of coolness.

Dust devils danced across the yard, scattering chickens, covering the porch and the dog with a thin layer of dust. He made no move to avoid the swirling dirt.

After lunch, being unable to finish her meal she placed the remains in a coffee can lid and put them on the bottom step. She stood for a moment uncertain what to do next, then turned back to the kitchen to wash up and figure out what to put together for the evening meal. She noted the lid was empty when she went to gather the eggs and secure the chickens for the night. There was no way to know if the dog or the chickens, who ran freely in the yard, had eaten the food. It puzzled the woman that the dog had not killed one to eat as he must be hungry by now.

Every time the woman had checked on the pan, the water was gone. But she never saw the dog take a drink. She looked around for something deeper, like a pot she could spare. How she wished it would move on, as she needed the pot, she had so few.

The dog and the woman eyed each other for a couple more days. He remained by the bush, leaving only for the scraps and the water. It became clear he had no intention of going, and she could not bring herself to chase him away.

At the end of the week, late in the evening she stepped out on the porch, eyed the dog for a few minutes before she seated herself on the top step. Clearing her throat, she called out, "Hey there, you worthless four-legged garbage disposal come on over here or get on with yourself." The dog focused on her face, pointing his ears in her direction. He got up and hesitantly moved toward her.

Stopping at the bottom step, he searched her face. A slight movement of his tail suggested a wag. "Well, for the lack of a better name, I am going to call you Mutt. So, Mutt, if you're going to stick around here, it's best we get a little acquainted." Snapping her fingers, she patted her knee. Mutt slowly climbed the steps keeping his eyes on hers, pausing for a minute before laying his head in her lap, then Mutt curled up in it and fell asleep.

The woman stayed that way, listening to the night sounds until her knee joints became stiff, and her back ached. She didn't want to wake the sleeping animal.

Before she retired for the night, the woman folded an old army blanket and placed it by the back door watching as the dog curled upon it. She went to bed content.

The rooster woke her as usual. Singing softly, she dressed, thinking I'll make buttermilk biscuits. They could bake while I tend the chickens. Dusting the flour from her hands she put the pan in the oven, humming as she went out to pet Mutt. The dog was gone.

Devastated, she couldn't stop crying as she went about the morning chores. She'd fed the chickens, but had she put out fresh water for them? She shouldn't have fed the dog. If you fed it, you keep it. If you keep it, you name it. If you give something a name, it will leave you.

Tears running down her cheeks, she pulled the burnt biscuits from the oven and scraped off the charred bottoms. She reached for the wild plum jam. She couldn't bring herself to open it. Instead, the woman sipped enough warm tea to ease the pain in her stomach. It did nothing to ease the pain in her heart. Then she heard scratching at the door.

Looking through the patched screen she saw the dog. Mutt looked at her face, from his mouth hung a dead rabbit. She opened the door and stepped out. The dog dropped the warm, motionless creature at her feet.

Stifling a scream, she shook off the dead animal, then dropped to her knees and hugged the dog that would not go away.

"We'll make it, won't we, Mutt" she whispered. "We'll make it."

Yipping and squirming he licked the tears from her face.

The woman had never skinned an animal in her life, much less killed one. She would starve first. In a flash of acceptance, the woman knew somehow before the sunset that day, she and Mutt would have rabbit stew.

PART II
SELECTED POETRY

Painting by Author 1968

THOUGHTS IN PASSING

I'm not much of a traveler,
but my mind is always on the go.
It goes where my body
never even thought of going.

I don't know where the time went,
but it did!
And it's going even faster now
that I'm getting slower.

I'm not sure I will live long enough
to do all the things
I still want to do.
What is amazing are the things
I've accomplished since
I legally became a Senior Citizen.

I can almost remember
when I knew it all.
Now I wish I could remember
if I knew anything at all!

If I had the chance to do it all over again,
would I do it the same way?
I suppose I still wouldn't know any better!

I've been young,
I've been middle-aged,

and now I'm "old-aged":
Don't tell me I don't know what I'm doing!
If there's one thing I've
learned through the "ages";
If I don't know something,
I find out.

Live my life over?
I'd want to talk about better options
before I decide.

The meaning of Life?
Good question.
I'm still asking it.

I'm not sure what's coming next,
but death holds no fear:
I'm much too curious about what
"next" is!

CONVERSATIONS OF THE HEART

Yesterday

Yesterday I watched a seagull circle the sky,
Then settle on the grass
Just beyond where I was sitting.
Not looking for food, as it ignored
The crust I tossed its way.
Nor did it seem concerned when
The sparrows fought over it.
It kept a wary eye on me,
As it worked its way
Just beyond the reach of my hand.

The gull did not move as I touched my cheek
Where the breeze
Brushed it as lightly as your kiss had been,
Then moved on
To rustle the leaves at my feet.

The Seagull waited, watching,
Just beyond my touch,
For what, I could not guess,
As you waited,
For what, I did not understand…
And that, too, was yesterday.

I remember you,

Your touch.
I remember the touch of you,
Your laughter, your silence,
And when it needed be your anger.

I remember the trees as you saw them.
I heard the wind as you heard it.
I feel the grass as you felt it.
But you are not here, only I.
I reach for you;
My hand caresses emptiness.
Memories fill the space.

Watching the seagulls play among the clouds
I remember the closeness
Of our silences and wish to hear it again
I wish for you, love,
And I wish for me.
It could have been my love.

Again, I watched a seagull flying, alone,
Then lighting on the grass;
Was content to be alone.
Where is yesterday?
It was here but a bit ago,
With you:
Now both are gone.

Flight

It danced lightly in the wind
Just beyond my hand;

Playing in the breeze, circling,
Before it fell at my feet.

It lay lightly fluttering as I watched,
Daring not to touch,
Should it go? Then it did,
Skipping with the breeze.

It was free, belonging no more to its past
Saying in ways that words cannot
That it belonged to no one. I let it be
Free, but not forgotten: the feather.

Remembering

I walk:
The breeze lifts my hair as gently as your hand;
It brushes my cheek as softly as your kiss.

We talk:
You answer not my words,
Only the thoughts of my heart.

I listen
To the echo of your laughter
In the laughter of the crowds

I walk, alone,
But you are with me:
I hear you whisper to me.

My heart
Follows you in my dreams,
And feels again your presence

Silently Listening

In silence, you creep in and tell me to listen,
And hear the trees as they move
To the music of the wind,
And you are there.
I hear you in the sound of footsteps,
A closing door;
You are everywhere.
I hear you in the echo of laughter,
In the melody of a song.
I hear you even in silence,
When I listen.

It's Been Said

Words fell helplessly to the floor,
Surrounding your feet....
You stumbled over them
As you moved beyond their sound.
And I stood helplessly where I was.
I can say no more,
Because it has already been said.

Along

Silence pounds my ears with noise,
Choking words that fight to be heard,
Screaming their presence; only I hear them.
You sleep; I am alone in the silence,
Frightened by its sound.

We spend time and talk,
But say nothing;
Depart,
Feeling empty,
And do not understand why.

Too Late

We will talk about this another time;
Saying goodbye, we hand up.
But we know we never will:
It is already too late.

Somewhere Else

You were already on your way to somewhere else.
You didn't bother to say goodbye;
You just didn't return.

It didn't matter that you went;
It mattered only
You didn't say you were going.

Anymore

I thought of you
While you were gone.
I thought of us,
And what we were,
And I missed you terribly.

Then I remembered
When you were here;
I remembered All that we weren't
And I didn't miss you anymore.

Empty Space

I reach out
To touch you;
My hand finds
Only space,
My heart,
Emptiness.
You are already out of reach.

Love came
And stayed but a moment;
Then it was gone.
I wasn't sure that it was
Until I felt the empty
Space it left.

Letting Go

Let's not get close enough to hold hands!
Just walk with me for a little while;
Share with me a laugh, a smile...
And when we come to the fork in the path,
Go your way, and wave to me as you go.

Had we walked holding hands,
One of us would have had to let go first.

The Endlessness

Time rushed on, not waiting, not looking back.
I, in my hurry to catch up, was lost in its flight,
And stumbling to a standstill, sat
Letting it go by, no longer caring
That I was not with it nor it with me,
Tired of the endlessness of it all.

PART III
FAMILY STORIES

ASHES, ASHES

Adults didn't play games, not even domino's. They sat around and talked—mostly about the weather. I had thought little about the 1930s until reading Angela's Ashes. A friend who also had read it, commented, can you imagine eating fried bread three times a day? I would have liked to have had fried bread. It would have been a welcome change from cornbread and milk three times a day. Fried bread? Maybe mom knew about it.

We had to save our fat, in a crock. It was used to make lye soap. Lye soap was what we used to wash our clothes. Lava soap, when we could afford it, was for hands and baths. I didn't know any other soap existed until I was eight. Ponds face soap was a cherished gift, we still used Lava everywhere else. I don't remember when Life boy replaced Lava for the bath. It was prettier, but it smelled worse.

The United States was in a depression in the 30s. Nobody had it good. No jobs. Even worse there were parts of the country that were plagued with drought. A wide belt which included Oklahoma and Texas had gone without rain, the life force of life itself for months on end. The farmers depended on rain to raise their cash crops and feed for their livestock. Rain didn't happen. Those were the dust bowl years as chronicled in the book, Grapes of Wrath.

My little corner of the world had not fully recovered from a shorter drought 1928 through 1930. Things were not good. Farmers, who had depended on the goodness of God, starved. They had to kill the livestock they couldn't afford feed. Mother Nature had not provided enough vegetation for the survival of the smallest of her wild animals, it was nothing to see a dead cottontail or jackrabbit, with scrawny vultures tearing it apart.

When there were cartridges for the .22 rifle, and a live rabbit was spotted and killed, we stewed it, not with carrots, potatoes, and onions, but string beans and turnips. In fact, I didn't know potatoes, carrots, and onions were used in stew until after we borrowed the weekly newspaper. I saw a stew recipe. It called for beef. As things got better, we fried the rabbits; they had more meat on their bones then, besides by then we had a good supply of lye soap.

Ashes, we saved them too. They were used in making the soap. Wood was the one thing in good supply. The peach trees, which needed more water than the mesquite was already dead, the mesquite was also dying.

Wood was plentiful. Soap we had. Water we didn't.

One year the rainfall was about three inches. "Hell," my Uncle Joe said. "I peed more than that last year."

"So," I said, "everybody pees and if everybody would just save their pee..." They sent me into the house. No one would discuss it with me. In fact, I was told not to mention it again. I didn't know if they were mad at me for taking part in an adult conversation or saying 'pee'. How was I to know? I was only five.

We bartered soap for flour. The flour came in cotton sacks with beautiful floral prints. Material for our school dresses. The chicken feed also came in lovely floral print sacks. After a while, Mom wouldn't let me feed the chickens anymore. I fed them too much.

I tried to get out of washing the dishes by using too much water. That didn't work, it only made things worse. I had to haul the water to wash the dishes. The pump was a quarter of a mile away. As if that wasn't already too much, I had to prime the pump too. It was a lot harder than pumping a trough full of water for the livestock.

Cornmeal came from our own corn. When we had any to spare, we took it to town to be ground. Sometimes, for an extra nickel, it was put in a white sack. If the sack didn't have to be saved, it became underwear for the girls. I don't remember what the boy's underwear was made of, or if they even wore any. I remember wondering if adults did.

As the drought and depression years added up, no jobs, no rain, little food, and hand-me-down clothing. The fun had all but stopped. There was little visiting and when company came there wasn't much talking, and the children didn't play *Ring Around Rosie* much. Because when we sang, 'ashes, ashes all fall down', we couldn't fall down. We couldn't get our clothes dirty. One good garment was all we had. We changed the song to A*shes, Ashes, Don't Fall Down,* and settled for a table game.

BEST FRIEND

Spike came to live with us in the summer of 1945. He was my four-year-old brother's best friend, in fact, his only friend. Johnny was the youngest of five, with a four-year separation in age from his nearest sibling. That didn't offer him much in playmates. When Johnny got to play with his older sisters, he had to play *House* and be the baby. By the time we made it to California in February of that year he rebelled, yelling at his sisters, "Go get yourself another baby."

There weren't any kids his age in the neighborhood we had moved to. His world had shrunk, confined by a white picket fence. In Texas, Johnny's early years were spent on a farm, his boundaries limitless. As long as he could see our house, he could go almost anywhere.

Johnny had many digging places and was content playing alone; making hills, rivers, and roads for his little red dump truck. Now, a 4 by 40-foot space between the house and a white picket fence that surrounded the front yard was the only place that was his.

"Spike is going to have supper with us tonight," Johnny announced one evening, "and he wants to sit right there," pointing at my chair.

"But that's my place," I protested. My place was on the corner nearest the stove as it was my job to keep the serving bowls filled. "I'm going to sit next to Spike," he said, "so, you'll have to sit on the other side of me."

Stuck in the middle made my job harder. Protesting did no good. Mom gave me that *just drop it* look.

Part of my duty was to serve up Johnny's plate. Now, Spike's plate too. He wanted his mashed potatoes in the center of his plate and only six peas around the edge. The gravy in the middle, never to drip over the sides.

"This is insane," I grumbled.

I had heard about Spike for a while now, but as a teenager, had paid little attention. I was too caught up learning about my new world. I'd heard how he had taken the evening newspaper before it was read and made a fleet of boats. He also broke an egg on the back steps to see if the steps were hot enough to fry an egg. He got the hose and drenched Diablo, our big, black cat. Using Johnny's digging spot for a toilet should have been the last straw. Why Mom hadn't banished him for that was beyond me. You didn't mistreat animals, for any reason, a hard and fast rule Mom drilled into us. That was my first encounter with the little monster. He even got my chair. A three-foot step ladder was not the most comfortable thing to sit on. I was not happy with the situation but trying to reason it out with Mom was useless.

In the second week of September, Johnny took Spikes' plate from the table, returning it to the counter. He looked at me, then pulled the step ladder away. "You can have your place back," he said. "Spike isn't going to live with us anymore. He is going to live with another little boy who needs a friend."

POCAHONTAS

Weeks after returning to California, my younger sister called. She had been doing family research and ask if I'd ever heard the story about being descendants of Pocahontas? I said yes but didn't take much stock in it. "Well, if you aren't sitting, you'd better," she said. Later she sent me pages of a convincing paper trail.

Our grandfather, L.N. Halbert is her descendant. The Halbert men had a long lineage of military officers, clergy, Judges, and Lawyers. One of the Halbert men had married into Pocahontas's lineage. Similar to the Halbert men, Pocahontas's ancestry was full of military, clergy, politicians and prominent businessmen. Having such notable ancestry, in both family lines are well documented.

As a child, over three hundred thirty years after Pocahontas, I rode my horse bareback, sometimes with a turkey feather in my hair. The feather soon blew away as I did not inherit the thick dark hair of my ancestor. I learned to swim in a river clothed or not. Always carried my hook, line, and sinker wrapped around a cork in my pocket along with a pocket knife. In season, I picked wild berries and nuts and spent as much time barefoot as the weather would allow. My father's sister, Becky, claimed I lived like an Indian and was as brown as one.

That was as close as I came to be an Indian. I lived in a house, with windows of glass, slept in beds covered with sheets and quilts. Pocahontas may have lived in a longhouse covered with animal skins. Those same skins covered her when she slept and used to make her clothes. If she rode horses, it was bareback. I pictured her walking barefooted on deer trails, picked wild berries and swam in the rivers and creeks. Pocahontas might have tucked flowers in her hair.

Over the twenty years of her short life, she sailed the Atlantic, was wined and dined in grand houses. They built those houses on cobblestone streets, a far cry from the deer trails and the muddy ruts of the wagon roads she had known in Virginia. The Rolfe's presented Pocahontas as an example of a "civilized savage" to the Royalty of England and was a guest at the Twelfth Night Christmas masque at Whitehall Palace in London. She became a celebrity in London society when introduced as an Indian Princess and the favorite daughter of the Indian King in America.

In an Indian village near Richmond, Virginia, Pocahontas was born. The year was 1595. Although Columbus had discovered this part of the world a little over a hundred years before, it took Sir Walter Raleigh in 1584 to discover and annexed Virginia, eleven years before her birth.

With the blessing and help of Queen Elizabeth I of England, Raleigh unsuccessfully tried to colonize North Carolina and Virginia. Few of the colony survived the first winter. Captain John Smith appeared on the scene in the next ten years and Lord De la Warr-Thomas West. At that time, there might have been less than twenty non-native Americans there. In 1600, about two hundred years later, the census of 1790 listed only 692 non-native Americans in all of Virginia.

Young men only courted young women within a day's horseback ride of their homes. Often limiting them to relatives, Indians, and blacks.

I had not realized that the slave trade was already part of the world export. In 1509, a Roman Catholic bishop proposed that each Spanish settler in the new world should bring a certain number of slaves. Coronado, in 1541 had already made tracks in New Mexico, Oklahoma, Texas, and Kansas territories. De Soto discovered the Mississippi River the same year. DeSoto had already looked Florida over. The Texas territory had been under the Spanish flag since 1519.

The Mayflower did not dock at Plymouth Rock until 1620 three years after Pocahontas's death. I find it mind-boggling to realize from this auspicious beginning in a small area of space and time; Pocahontas was to become part of history. In the same year she was born, across the ocean, the first heels appeared on shoes. England would outlaw a bow as a weapon of war, and Shakespeare wrote *A Mid Summers Night's Dream*. He wrote Romeo and Juliet the previous year. Also, Sir Francis Drake and Sir John Hopkins left Plymouth on their last voyage. Sir Walter Raleigh was exploring the Orinoco River in Venezuela.

I wonder if Pocahontas even learned to read and write? The lead pencil had been in use for a hundred years. Gutenberg invented the moveable press and printed the Bible in 1455. During that time, I guess educating women was not on the priority list of humanity.

Captain John Smith may have been a part of the 120 colonists who came in 1606 with the Virginia Company of London by Royal Charter as he would write in 1608 a book titled, The True Relations of Virginia, in 1612 and, A Map of Virginia.

John Smith also wrote of being saved by Pocahontas, but his first account of this he mentioned only four Indians. Sixteen years later, he would add a few more Indians and the Pocahontas tale. She had been dead for seven years when this writing became public. His is the only account of this "happening". None of the other Virginia colonists mentioned the Pocahontas incident in their letters home. This well may be one of Captain John Smith's embellishments. With Disney's help, making her as popular as Shakespeare and as well known.

John Rolfe came later as he was in Bermuda in 1609 where his first wife died in childbirth. The child, a daughter, was named Bermuda. John Rolfe would come to Virginia and become a tobacco farmer. He married Pocahontas on April 4, 1614 (she was nineteen). Their son John was born in 1615 in Virginia. Pocahontas would travel to England in that year where she was presented to the English Court by Lord De La Warr Thomas West, who must have come with the Virginia Company of London or soon after as he was Governor Lieutenant of that colony. The State of Delaware was named in his honor.

Other notables and events that would become landmarks of history, was Cervantes, the noted author of Don Quixote, Part I and Part II. The Catholic Church prohibited Galileo from any further scientific study. The Notre Dame Cathedral at Antwerp was finished after 200 hundred plus years. James I sold peerage titles, to improve his financial situation, Stuart collars became fashionable for men and women.

Pocahontas would never return to America. In 1616 she died of unknown cause on her way to the ship to take Rolfe's back to Virginia. She died on March 20, at Gravesend, England where she is buried. That same year the playwright Shakespeare also died. Over three hundred years later the world still knows them well.

She left a year-old son John, and from this line produced many notables, John Randolph of Roanoke, and Edith Bolling Galt, the second wife of Woodrow Wilson, and my grandfather, L.N. Halbert.

www.ingramcontent.com/pod-product-compliance
Lightning Source LLC
Chambersburg PA
CBHW041032170626
46815CB00005B/295